THE
LONGEST
JOURNEY
IN THE
WORLD

Holt, Rinehart and Winston, Inc.
New York, Toronto, London, Sydney

Copyright © 1970 by Holt, Rinehart and Winston, Inc.
Published simultaneously in Canada
Printed in the United States of America
Library of Congress Catalog Number: 73-107087

a Bill Martin INSTANT Reader

THE
LONGEST
JOURNEY
IN THE
WORLD

by William Barrett Morris
with pictures by Betty Fraser
& handlettering by Ray Barber

One morning as the sun was coming up,

a little caterpillar said to himself,

" I am

going

on a

long

journey."

He crawled

and he crawled   and he crawled.

He crawled over a high mountain.

He crawled into a deep valley.

He crawled around a huge castle.

He crawled up a high wall.

He crawled across a wide river.

He crawled under an iron fence.

He crawled over a fallen tree.

He crawled past
a sleeping
dragon.

He   crawled   through

a dense forest.

He crawled and he crawled

and he crawled.

That night as the sun was going down,
the little caterpillar wondered
how far he had come. So he
climbed a tall Chinaberry tree to look back.

"I am truly amazed," he said to himself.
"This is the longest journey in the world."